THE SNOW MAZE

Joe discovers a secret behind the lonely gate on his way to school. But will anybody believe him?

Jan Mark is one of the most distinguished authors of books for young people and has twice been awarded the Carnegie Medal. Her many titles for Walker Books include *Taking the Cat's Way Home* and *Lady Long-legs* as well as the Walker picture books *Fur, Strat and Chatto* (Winner of the 1990 Mother Goose Award), *Fun with Mrs Thumb, This Bowl of Earth, The Midas Touch* and *The Tale of Tobias*. Jan lives in Oxford.

"A highly imaginative and beautifully scripted tale." *Books for Keeps and The Reading and Language Information Centre*

Books by the same author

Lady Long-legs
Taking the Cat's Way Home

For older readers

The Eclipse of the Century
The Lady with Iron Bones
Mr Dickens Hits Town
Nothing To Be Afraid Of
The Sighting
They Do Things Differently There
Thunder and Lightnings

Picture books

The Midas Touch
The Tale of Tobias

Jan Mark

The Snow Maze

Illustrations by Jan Ormerod

WALKER BOOKS
AND SUBSIDIARIES

LONDON · BOSTON · SYDNEY · AUCKLAND

For Joe Falker
J.M.

First published 1992 by
Walker Books Ltd, 87 Vauxhall Walk
London SE11 5HJ

This edition published 2005

2 4 6 8 10 9 7 5 3 1

Text © 1992 Jan Mark
Illustrations © 1992 Jan Ormerod

The right of Jan Mark and Jan Ormerod to be identified as author
and illustrator respectively of this work has been asserted by them
in accordance with the Copyright, Designs and Patents Act 1988

This book has been typeset in Garamond

Printed and bound in Great Britain by J.H. Haynes & Co. Ltd

British Library Cataloguing in Publication Data:
a catalogue record for this book is
available from the British Library

ISBN 1-84428-968-0

www.walkerbooks.co.uk

Contents

The Key

On the way to school Joe found
a key. It was in the long grass,
so he did not see it. He kicked it
with his toe.

It flew into the air
and clinked upon a stone.

Then he saw it.

Joe picked up the key. He held it
in the air and turned it round. It was
not like the key of Joe's front door.
It was like the key of the back door,
but it was twice as long and three
times heavier.

"Maybe a giant dropped this key,"
Joe said.

He took the key to school and
showed it to Irrum.

"Maybe a giant dropped it," said Joe.

"Can I hold it?" Irrum said.

Joe let Irrum hold the key while he counted. It was a special way of counting. "One-elephant, two-elephant, three-elephant, four-elephant, five-elephant."

That was five whole seconds.

Then he took it back. Other people came to look. Joe let each one hold it for five seconds, while he counted elephants. They thought it was a good key.

Then Akash came along. Joe tried to hide the key, but Akash saw it.

Akash laughed. He always laughed at Joe.

"That key is no good," Akash said. "Keys are no good unless they open something."

Then everyone laughed at Joe, except Irrum.

Everyone did what Akash did, except Irrum.

When everyone had gone away, Irrum said, "I think it is a good key. Perhaps it is magic. Perhaps it will open the lonely gate."

The Lonely Gate

Joe passed the lonely gate when he went home from school.

It stood on its own between two gateposts.

On the other side of the gate was a grassy field, but Joe could get on to the field without going through the gate. There was no wall to keep him out. The wall had fallen down and the gate stood all alone. That was why it was called the lonely gate. No one ever went through it. It was locked.

The gate was made of wood. Ivy climbed up it.

Joe moved the ivy leaves and underneath there was a keyhole. He put his key in the lock and turned it.

The key clicked. The lock squeaked.
Joe pushed. The ivy tried to hold
shut the gate, but Joe pushed harder.

The ivy let go. The hinges
screeched. The gate opened.

On the other side of the gate was
the grassy field, with a path in it.
Joe looked at the path. It went
round and round, backwards and
forwards, in the grassy field. He
had never seen it before.

Joe looked round the gatepost at
the grassy field. There was no path.

The path was there only if he went through the gate. Perhaps Irrum was right, and he had found a magic key.

Joe began to walk along the path. He walked ten steps and then the path turned. Joe turned too.

Now he was walking back to the gate, but before he got there the path turned again. This time it went round the grassy field, but before it got back to the gate it turned again, and Joe turned too.

Joe and the path went backwards and forwards, round and round, and when the path stopped at last, Joe was right in the middle of the field.

He knew it was time to go home or his mum would worry, so he ran back, along the path, round and round, backwards and forwards, until he came to the gate.

He went out of the gate and locked it. He looked round the gatepost. There was no path.

Irrum was right. He had found a magic key.

The Lost Maze

When Joe went to school next day he passed the lonely gate. He looked at the grassy field. There was no path. He opened the gate with his key.

The path was there.

He locked the gate again.

At school, he said to Miss, "What do you call it when a path goes round and round, backwards and forwards, all folded up?"

"I think that's a maze," said Miss.

"No it's not," Tim said. "I went in a maze with my mum. It had high hedges. We got lost."

"Not all mazes have hedges," Miss said. "Some are made of turf. Turf is grass."

"How can you get lost in grass?" Tim said.

"You don't get lost in a turf maze," Miss said. "It's a magic pattern. You run along the path."

"Boring," said Akash. He did not believe in magic.

"How did you know about the maze, Joe?" Miss asked.

Joe did not want to tell. "I saw a picture," he said.

"Once there was a turf maze near this school," Miss told them. "But it was lost, long ago."

"That was careless," Akash said.

"How can you lose a maze?" Tim asked.

"Perhaps a farmer ploughed over it," Irrum said.

"I know where that maze is," Joe said to himself.

After school he went to the lonely gate and opened it with his key.

 Then he saw Akash, down by the pillar box, so he closed the gate and locked it behind him. He ran round the path to the middle of the maze.

Akash stood in the road and shouted.

"Why are you going round and round like that?"

"I'm running my maze," Joe said.

"I can't see any maze," Akash said. "I think you're mad."

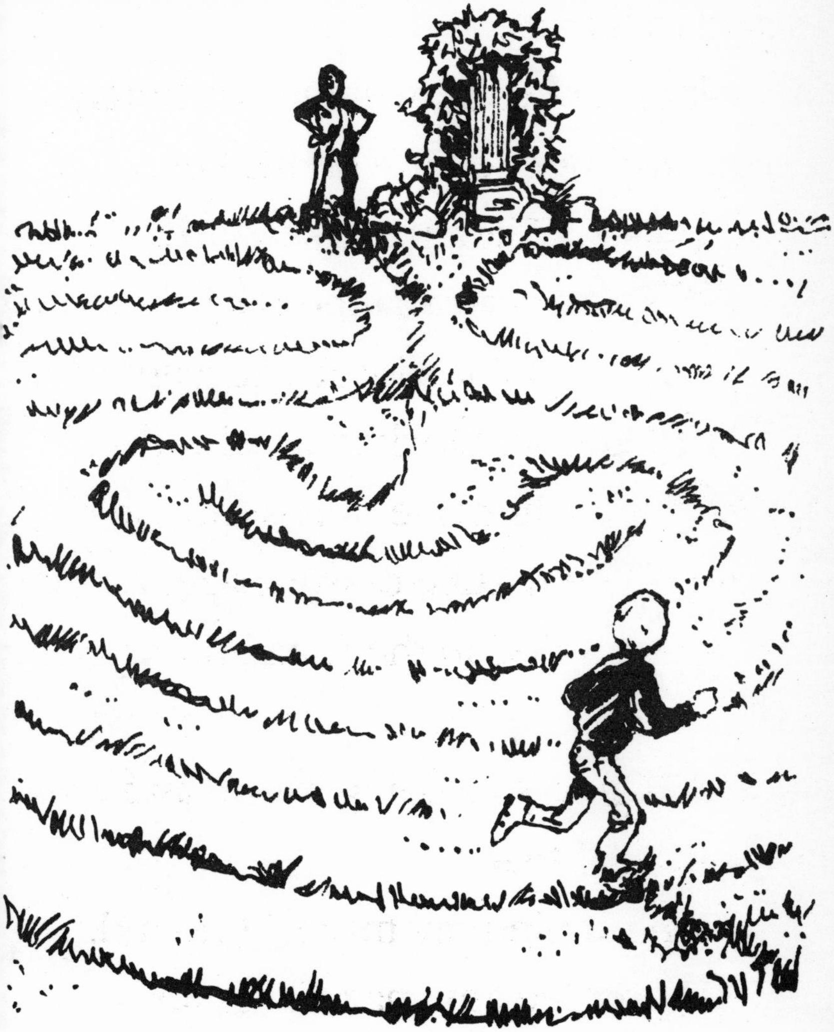

Joe stepped out of the maze and went over to stand by Akash. He looked back. The maze was not there.

"It's a secret maze," Joe said. "I'm the only one who can see it."

"Huh! You are mad," Akash said.

The Secret Maze

Akash was big and strong. He was not a bully, but people did what he told them to.

Tim was not a bully, either, but he wanted to be like Akash.

When Akash said something, Tim said it too.

Next day, at school, Akash said,
"Joe's mad. He can see things that
are not there."

"Joe's mad,"
said Tim.
"Joe's bad."
He did not think
Joe was bad, but
he liked the sound
of it. "Mad Joe,
bad Joe, sad Joe,"
the others shouted.
"Joe's got a maze,"
Akash said.
"Mazy Joe!"

"Joe's mazy," said Tim. "Joe's crazy."

"Mazy, crazy, lazy Joe," the others shouted. They all ran round and round in the playground, pretending to be Joe.

"This is what Joe does," Akash said, and the others followed him.

Irrum did not run or shout.

"Stupid people," Irrum said, and stood still, while the others ran about.

She stood on the edge of the playground, but Joe was in the middle. The others ran rings round him. People pushed him as they went past.

"Crazy Joe!" Akash shouted.

Joe did not want to be like Akash, big and strong. He wanted to be like Irrum, small and brave.

At home time Joe ran from school and opened the lonely gate. Then he ran his secret maze.

Akash told the others where he

went. They followed Joe, but Joe
had his key, and they could not go
through the gate into the maze.
They stood in the road and laughed
at Joe, running round and round,
backwards and forwards. They
could not see the maze.

Tim said that Joe was making it up.

Sometimes they all came and ran about on the grassy field, but only Joe could see the maze, because he had gone through the gate. It was his secret.

The Invisible Maze

Next day when Joe came to school, Akash and Tim shouted, "Mad, sad, bad Joe!"

"Mazy, crazy, lazy Joe!" the others shouted, and ran rings round Joe in the middle of the playground.

Irrum stood beside him.

"Crazy, lazy, mazy," Akash yelled.

"Stupid people," Irrum said.

Miss came out to see what they were doing.

"We're playing mazes, Miss," said Tim.

Miss laughed. "That's good," she said. She could not hear what they were shouting.

At break Joe stayed indoors and helped Miss find lost scissors.
At lunch time he hid in the toilets.
At afternoon play it rained and they could not go out. Miss sent them to the hall to run about. The maze game started again. Joe sat under a table and held his key.

Irrum went up to Akash.

Akash was yelling. "Mad, sad. Crazy, mazy."

"I'd rather be crazy than nasty," Irrum said. "I'd rather be sad than stupid."

"You don't want to be like mazy Joe," Tim said.

"I don't want to be like you," said Irrum, and she did not run away.

When people were rude to Tim and Akash, they ran away quickly. Irrum just stood, and stared and glared. Tim and Akash went on shouting, but they did not shout so loudly.

Joe wished he were small and brave, like Irrum, but he was only small.

After school, he went away alone, and opened the gate with his key.

He ran his maze, all alone.

One morning Joe saw Irrum standing by the lonely gate.

Irrum said, "Show me your maze, Joe."

"No," said Joe.

"But I believe you," Irrum said. "I don't think you're making it up."

Then Joe remembered how Irrum had told him that the key might open the lonely gate. He remembered how Irrum stood beside him when the others played mazes.

"All right," said Joe, and he
unlocked the gate.

"Can you see the maze?" Joe said.

"Yes," said Irrum.

"Run round it then," Joe said, in
case she was pretending, and Irrum
ran along the path. She could see
it too.

Joe looked round the gatepost at the grassy field. All he could see was Irrum, running, backwards and forwards, round and round. The maze was invisible.

Every day after that, Joe and Irrum unlocked the lonely gate, when no one was looking. They ran the maze.

The others came and stood in the road and laughed. They could see Irrum and Joe, but the maze was invisible.

The Frost Maze

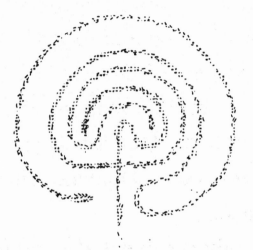

One morning it was cold and there was white frost on the grassy field. When Irrum and Joe unlocked the gate and ran the maze, they left footprints.

No one else was there.

Afterwards Joe locked the gate and they looked round the gatepost. The maze was invisible, but the footprints were still there, running round and round, backwards and forwards.

"Let's show the others," Irrum said.

"No," said Joe.

"But now they will believe you," Irrum said.

Joe thought about this all day.

He wanted to be believed, but he wanted to keep his secret maze.

At home time some snowflakes
fell. Joe and Irrum ran to the grassy
field and the footprints were still
there, in the frost. They had not
melted, but the snow was beginning
to cover them up.

Joe unlocked the gate and they
started to run the maze, round and
round, backwards and forwards.

The snow got deeper and deeper, so they ran the maze again, to keep the path open.

The others came along. They stood in the road and watched. Then they ran on to the grassy field.

"Stop them," Irrum said. "Their footprints will spoil our footprints and we will lose the maze."

Joe stood still.
He thought.

"Go back!"
he shouted.
"I'll let you in
through the
lonely gate."

The others went back. Joe unlocked the gate and let them in.

"Can you see the maze?" Irrum said, and they all said, "Yes".

"Then follow me," said Joe, and they all ran the maze, one behind the other. When they got to the middle they turned round and went back to the gate. But the snow was

still falling, so they turned round
and ran the maze again.

And then Irrum said, "Look!"

There in the road was her mum,
and Joe's mum, and Akash's granny
and Tim's dad. Miss was there too.
They had come to look for the
children, all the mums and dads and
grannies.

They stood in a row and looked at the grassy field. Now it was a field of snow.

"What can you see?" called Joe, and they all called back, "We can see a maze!"

It was not a turf maze any longer. It was a snow maze. Everyone could see it now.

The Sand Maze

The snow fell faster and thicker.

"What shall we do?" said Miss. "The children have found the lost maze. We must not lose it again."

Tim's dad was a builder. He ran through the snow to fetch sand in a barrow.

Then he followed the footprints, backwards and forwards, round and round the maze, and poured sand into them.

Right away the snow covered the sand.

"But when it melts," said Irrum's mum, "the sand will still be there."

"And the maze will still be there," Akash said.

He laughed. He was not laughing at Joe, he was laughing because he was pleased about the maze, so Joe laughed, too.

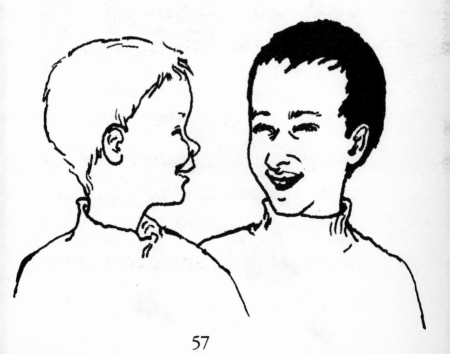

Akash was right. When the snow melted, the sand maze was still there on the grassy field. People came with spades and cut out the path, and so the maze was there for always, and everyone could see it.

But it began at the lonely gate. The gate was locked and Joe had the key.

One day, when no one was looking, he unlocked the lonely gate for the last time. He left it standing open, so anyone could run the maze whenever they wanted to. It was not a secret maze any more, and the gate was no longer lonely.

Everyone was pleased because the children had found the lost maze.

"Joe found it," Irrum said.

"How did you find it, Joe?" asked Miss.

"Irrum told me where to look," said Joe.

"How did Irrum know where to look?" asked Miss.

"I just told him to open the lonely gate," Irrum said. She did not tell about the key.

After school Joe took the key and went back to the place where he had found it. He hid the key in the long grass.

One day the maze might be lost again.

One day, someone else might find the key.

other 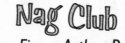 for you to enjoy

Cool as a Cucumber

Michael Morpurgo • Tor Freeman

Peter gets more than he bargained for when he starts digging the school's Jubilee vegetable garden!

Nag Club

Anne Fine • Arthur Robins

When expert parent-nagger Lola forms a club to show her classmates how to get round their parents, the results aren't quite what she expected…

Taking the Cat's Way Home

Jan Mark • Paul Howard

New boy William seems to have it in for Jane, and the only way she can escape him after school is to follow her cat along the wall, into the unknown…

Star Striker Titch

Martin Waddell • Russell Ayto

Little Titch wants to play a big part in the school World Cup – if only he could get on the pitch!

Care of Henry

Anne Fine • Paul Howard

When Hugo's mum goes into hospital, he must decide who he wants to stay with. The key to it all is Henry, his dog.